Peter Magers

Dinosaur Monster Truck Race

Illustrated by

Peter Magers and Windel Eborlas

Balboa Press books may be ordered through booksellers or by contacting:

Balboa Press
A Division of Hay House
1663 Liberty Drive
Bloomington, IN 47403
www.balboapress.com.au
1 (877) 407-4847

ISBN: 978-1-5043-2112-9 (sc)
978-1-5043-2113-6 (e)

Print information available on the last page.

Balboa Press rev. date: 04/03/2020

BALBOA.PRESS
A DIVISION OF HAY HOUSE

Dedication

To our adventurous and creative, Ethan and Isaac who helped co-author this book. We love you to the end of the universe and back our little ninjas.

About the author

Peter Magers is a storyteller. Every night, he crafts up new bedtime stories, based on his children's choice of characters. He is best known for fantasy, sci-fi and fairy tales. He also tells non-fiction stories, weaving in subjects ranging from astronomy to nature to history. Surely the children's favourite part of the day is bedtime?!

Far, far away, in another galaxy, there is a planet that looks like Earth. The planet is covered with water and land just like Earth. There are three islands joined together in the middle by giant rocky mountains.

Dinosaurs live on these islands. Not your normal, everyday dinosaurs but monster truck dinosaurs.

The giant rocky mountains in the middle were so big, the dinosaurs from the different islands never saw each other.

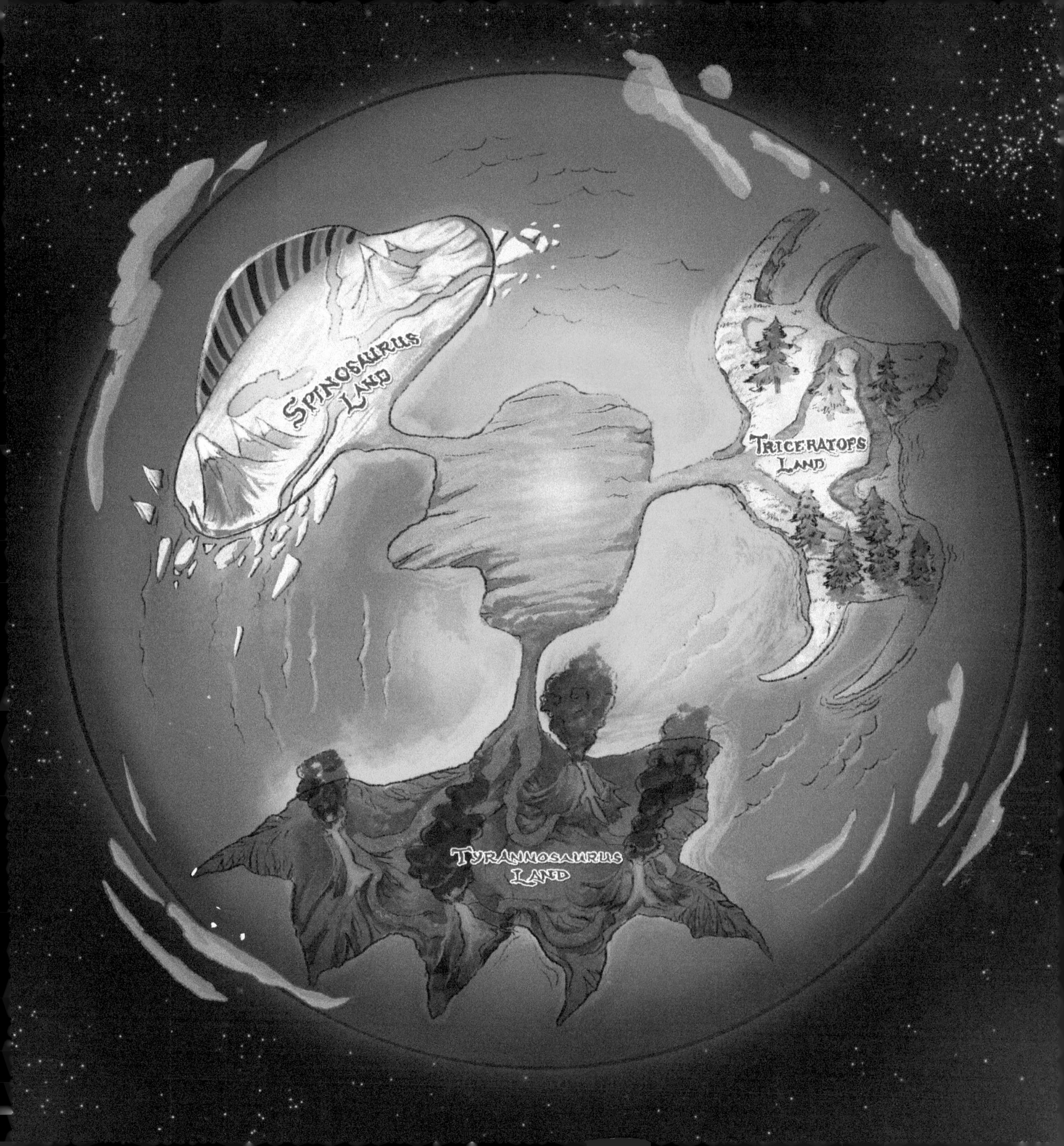
Spinosaurus
Land
Triceratops
Land
Tyrannosaurus
Land

One day, there was a big earthquake that flattened the giant rocky mountains. The dinosaurs started exploring into this new land.

T-Rex left Tyrannosaurus Land, Spiny left Spinosaurus Land, and Tops left Triceratops Land. They bumped into each other at a cross road.

"Hello, I am Tops, and I am the fastest dinosaur on the planet."

"Hmmmph, I am faster than you," roared Spiny.

"I am definitely the fastest!" T-Rex boomed.

"Let's race to find out," said T-Rex.

Spiny and Tops happily agreed.

The Dinosaur Monster Truck Race will drive through all the islands, through forests, volcanoes and water.

Racer number one is T-Rex. He is a fire dinosaur. Fast, Angry and Super Powerful. He farts flames out his butt.

Racer number two is Spiny. He is a water dinosaur. He can surf on water. He is Light, Speedy and Fierce. He burps stinky gas.

Racer number three is Tops. He is a forest dinosaur. He is Quick, Happy and Mischievous. He makes giant poo-poos.

T-Rex

Spiny

Tops

The Dinosaur Monster Trucks come together at the starting line. They all looked at one another and growled.

"You better not get in my way," growls T-Rex.

"You will be eating my dust," says Tops.

"You won't even see me because I'll be so far ahead in the race," boasts Spiny.

Secretly, they each have tricks to help them win the race.

Traffic lights change from red to yellow and yellow to green. And the dinosaurs are off.

They race through Triceratops Land. Tops takes the lead. His Triceratops friends cheer for him, "Go, Tops! Go!"

As T-Rex and Spiny catch up, Tops starts wiggling his butt and smelly monster poos plop onto the road.

"Yuck!" yells Spiny and T-Rex.

T-Rex got poo all over his tyres, slowing him down. Spiny has poo in his face and eyes. He cannot see where he is going and smashes into a tree. Bang!

Tops speeds ahead, laughing.

T-Rex cleans the poo off his tyres and starts racing after Tops. Spiny wipes the poo from his eyes and is also back in the race.

They arrive at the tallest mountains on the planet. Tops and T-Rex are side by side in the lead and Spiny is just behind them. "Get up there faster! Faster!" they tell themselves. They pant and grunt all the way up.

At the top, they let out a "Woo Hoo!" and start rolling down faster and faster, onto T-Rex Land. Volcanoes erupting, lava overflowing, the Dinosaur Monster Trucks feel hot. T-Rex rolls straight over lava covered tracks.

Spiny and Tops jump and hop, "Ow! Ow! Hot! Hot! Hot!" they scream as the lava burn their tyres.

T-Rex lets out an explosive fart, and a flame shoots out of his butt, propelling him even further in front.

"That's disgusting," says Spiny.

"The stink is horrible," says Tops.

As they enter Spinosaurus Land, T-Rex is so far ahead, it looks like he will win the race.

Tops is in second place and Spiny is coming in last.

The Dinosaur Monster Trucks must swim across water to finish the race. T-Rex and Tops dive right in and start spinning their tyres, but do not go very fast.

Spiny arrives at the water, turns around and lets out a huge burp. He surfs like a speed boat along the surface of the water. Spiny overtakes T-Rex and Tops and crosses the finish line to win the race!

It is now time for the awards ceremony.

The speaker booms: "Let's hear a huge dinosaur roar for our racers. In third place, we have Tops." The crowd roars.

"In second place, we have T-Rex." The crowd roars again.

"And the winner of the Dinosaur Monster Truck Race is Spiny." The crowd goes into a frenzy, roaring and cheering.

The dinosaurs climb up the podium to receive their medals. They nudge playfully, congratulating each other.

As a treat, the Dinosaur Monster Trucks get a free car wash as they are very dirty from the race. They finally get to relax.

T-Rex says, "Let's have this race again next year and see who wins."

A Pteranodon flies overhead and screeches, "I will challenge you to a flying race, haha."

The Dinosaur Monster Trucks look up in wonderment, "what is this creature???"

Printed in the USA
CPSIA information can be obtained
at www.ICGtesting.com
LVHW060253281123
765134LV00027B/1708